CW01663954

Poems FOR TITUS

Yvonne Bowerman

Poems for Titus

Republished 2024

Published by

Sophos Books Ltd.

Croydon

Surrey

sophosbooks.com

All Scriptures, unless otherwise stated, are taken from The Holy Bible, New International Version.

ISBN 978-1-905669-91-2

Cover design by Tope Enoch

Printed in England

I dedicate this book to the glory of God
and in memory of
Bishop Titus Olugbenga David
(7 March 1956 - 8 February 2002)

Contents

I Give Thanks...

I THANK GOD for choosing and loving me, and for His gifting of poetry and song.

I thank my parents for their love and care throughout my life and for telling me about Jesus.

I would like to thank my team of helpers and encouragers for making this project possible.

My warmest thanks to my husband, Richard, who has always been there for me, encouraging me in everything I do. He has been supportive, kind and patient during this time, giving me total freedom to devote myself to writing Poems For Titus and for giving his time to proof reading.

Without Thelma's skills of not only reading my handwriting, but also putting the manuscript on disc, I would not have finished this book so quickly. She is not only my sister in Christ and a dear friend, but she is also my partner in writing *Poems For Titus*. A big thank you to her for so willingly doing this work without complaint even when I altered things around. Thanks also go to Dave, Thelma's husband, who has given us both his support and love for this project.

Loving thanks to Ronke for her ideas and contribution.

Most special thanks to the late Reverend Vincent Onwukanjo of *Reconciler Evangelical Ministries*, London who became an instant encourager to me from the moment we first met.

Finally, thank you to everyone who has encouraged me with my poetry writing since I first started exercising my gift.

Introduction

MY HUSBAND RICHARD, and I, first met Ronke and Titus by chance, although on reflection, we now believe it was a God-led situation as we have all enjoyed and learnt so much through this relationship.

We had read of a vegetarian restaurant in Brixton that had won an award for its beautiful food and for making wonderful fresh fruit cocktails from freshly blended fruits. Although we are not vegetarian, we love the food and decided to try this restaurant, which we then discovered in the basement of a large London church.

After lunch Richard suggested that we look at the church. We were on the steps as members of *Christ's Family Church* came out from their service, so we stood to one side to let them pass.

One of the members spoke to us and asked if he could help. We told him that we'd just had lunch and wanted to see the inside of the church. He invited us in, we were hesitant, but he was insistent.

He then took us by surprise when he said, "You must come in to meet our Bishop."

My reply was, "Oh no, we are not here to meet the Bishop." Richard and I felt slightly uncomfortable at that point.

Bishop Titus and Ronke walked towards us, Ronke speaking to Richard whilst Titus asked me where we came from, why we were there, and what our church was like.

Bishop Titus showed interest and wanted to know more. He eventually asked if he could come to our church. Richard said, "Please come." I was a little in awe of my husband asking a Bishop to visit us and the church, but consoled myself at that point by thinking, *I'm sure he won't come.*

God and Titus had other ideas and in due course a date was arranged for him to visit us in order to attend the 6.30pm service at *St. Michael the Archangel.* It was a two-hour journey from Brixton and a tight schedule for him following his own service at Christ's Family Church.

He was suffering from jet lag, having recently journeyed home from Nigeria. A brother in Christ, Jacob, from *Christ's Family Church,* drove him and after a quick snack of homemade soup and bread at our home, we went to our church. I had previously arranged for seats to be reserved for us as I knew we would be a little late.

I remember Titus's astonishment as he saw the number of cars parked on the side of the road, as well as in the large car park. Jacob shouted "Revival!" as we approached our isolated country church.

At the end of the service the whole congregation filed passed shaking hands with Titus and Jacob. Titus met our Vicar, Brian Meardon, and they hugged each other warmly on sight and later Titus met two of Brian's sons, Mark and Trevor, and they had a long talk together.

As we drove back to our home for a snack and coffee, Titus confided in me that he had, in the past, thought that only London churches were expanding and growing. He now believed that God wanted him to see the growth of a country church and our very enthusiastic vicar, Brian, who worked along similar lines to himself.

Our friendship developed after this first meeting and I asked Titus if I could do anything to help with his work. He suggested that I collect Bibles, Christian books, and clothing. I placed an advertisement in our monthly church magazine and was astonished at the result. We were inundated with many books and clothes, which Richard and I stored at home, taking them eventually to Brixton in carloads. We off-loaded them into Titus's family car. Over time, we would make occasional visits to their home in Peckham for the same purpose.

We exchanged lots of telephone calls with Titus. His family visited and stayed with us for a few days to rest and enjoy the freedom of the countryside. Melody, Rachael, and Damilola wanted to fulfil their ambition to ride, and they achieved this at a local riding school which delighted them.

On one occasion, Ronke and Titus brought some

friends with them to visit us. We had been given several boxes of hymn books for Nigeria and the Reverend Esther and Bishop Yomi Isijola came to collect them for their mission work. We enjoyed a beautiful day with all of them.

I loved writing poetry and Titus encouraged me in this. Often, when I wrote to him, I would enclose a poem or two, which he sometimes used for the Church Bulletin which pleased me. On one occasion, when we were together, the subject of 'our wills' came up and Richard said, "I don't know what I will do with all of Yvonne's poetry that she has written." Titus said, "Give it all to me." I decided then, to copy some of my poems out into a small notebook as a gift for him. Later he rang me to say that he could clearly see my gifting and loved them, and that he would use some of them explaining that one in particular had "spoken" to him.

On another occasion when we visited *Christ's Family Church,* the Reverend Hugh Osgood was preaching. As we sat down, I opened the Bulletin and was astonished to see one of my poems printed on the back page. This was later read out to the congregation, and I felt myself blushing. When the Rev. Osgood started to speak, he said that he need not have written his sermon, because it was all in my poem! Was this a coincidence or a "God-incidence," as our Vicar, Brian, would say? There did seem to be definite link between ourselves and the David family and church. Every visit was a delight.

There are so many members of *Christ's Family*

Church, and others, who have welcomed us, loved us, cared for us, entertained us and nourished us both spiritually and physically. Unfortunately, I do not know them all by name. Richard and I are privileged to have enjoyed the friendship of these wonderful brothers and sisters in Christ.

Titus came to our home once to speak to some of our Christian brothers and sisters about his work, his hope for unity worldwide in the Body of Christ and more relationships were made that day.

I believe that 'unity within the Body of Christ Worldwide' was 'beginning' as our relationship with each other and our friends was growing.

- Yvonne Bowerman

The Task Ahead Is Never As Great As The Power Behind Us!

IT WAS THE morning of the 7th of March 2002. I telephoned Ronke to see how she was. She said, "It would have been Titus's birthday today."

After the telephone call, I started thinking about Titus and the fact that he would have been celebrating today. I remembered his birthday party that we attended just a year ago, when the whole of *Christ's Family Church* celebrated with him. We had a wonderfully happy day. I remember thinking how much Titus enjoyed his own family, the church family and invited guests. He was so full of love and happiness wanting everyone to be filled in the same way.

Into my mind came a small idea. Wouldn't it be wonderful if I could write a small book of poetry in 'Memory of Titus'. I had discussed with Titus some time ago, the idea of my writing a book of verse. He had encouraged me to do this, but somehow, it never seemed to be the right time.

I have written poems for many years. Creating the poems fills my heart with joy. Some had been used for friends at an appropriate moment, in our church magazine and collections of poems by different poets, which had been published. One or two had found their way into monthly magazines, but now I had a sense of purpose, to write *Poems for Titus*. What a privilege it would be for me to do this for him.

At the reception, after Titus's funeral, Richard and I had sat next to a gentleman who asked us how we met Ronke and Titus. He told me that he was very interested in poetry, songwriting, and drama, and that he helped others in this way with their creativity. I told him about my writing, and he offered to look at some of my poems and help me with them. I posted a few poems later to Rev. Vincent Onwukanjo.

It was on the evening of Titus' birthday that Rev. Vincent telephoned me to say that he had received the poems and had enjoyed reading them. We talked for a while, and I told him that it would have been Titus's birthday that very day. I mentioned the idea of *Poems For Titus* and he said he would help in any way that he could. He loved the idea. This encouragement gave me the confidence to put the plan into action.

After Titus's funeral I had composed a poem for *Christ's Family Church*. I had given it to Thelma, a sister in Christ, who was at the funeral with us. Quite unexpectedly, she called on us to present me with this poem, beautifully arranged on her computer. She gave it to me saying, "I loved it so much that I framed it."

I explained to her that I had decided to write *Poems for Titus* and without hesitation she said, "Let me do the typing for you." Thelma's husband, Dave, said, "I'll back you with this idea in any way I can."

Within two days, I had the embryo of an idea and now there were three willing helpers. My husband, Richard, wanted to be included as 'mistake spotter' and so my team was complete. The idea had grown into a 'workable project'.

I started this book on Titus's birthday, which was a wonderful day to start. The words flowed and on each of the mornings that followed I couldn't wait to get started. Thelma's fingers danced across the keys as she kept pace with me. The idea was becoming reality.

Opening Chapter

BISHOP TITUS DAVID was born on 7 March 1956 in Onse, Nigeria to Alice and David Fadairo. He spent his early childhood in Ilesha but later moved to Ibadan, with his parents, where he was educated.

He got 'Born Again' in 1969 and in January 1975, he dedicated his life to the Lord's service through the ministry of Gospel Group, the youth group of the Oritamefa Baptist Church in Ibadan.

His ministry started when he was appointed to lead the Gospel singers which was the ministry of the Gospel Group.

Between 1980 and 1983 he served as one of the youngest members of the Church Council of Oritamefa Baptist Church. He also pioneered the launch of the highly acclaimed Christian projects like 'Living Spring Musical Festival' and 'Gospel Music Promotions'.

Early in 1986 he joined the New Covenant Church in Ibadan and later that year moved to London and helped to pioneer the New Covenant Church in London.

In 1988 he established his own ministry, Christ's Family Church. On 6 February 1999, The International Ministerial Council of Great Britain consecrated him as a Bishop.

His passion and mission in life was to promote love and unity in the Body of Christ worldwide.

Titus and Aderonke got married on the 4th August 1984 and have three lovely daughters; Melody, Rachael and Damilola.

Bishop Titus David died tragically in a shooting incident in Nigeria on the 8th of February 2002.

(Culled from the Funeral Pamphlet)

Titus's Dream

AT THE HEART of Titus was his mission, his dream, and vision for unity. He wanted the whole world of Christian believers to become one powerful Body of Christ. He worked hard to achieve what seemed to most of us to be an impossible task. It was with great sadness that we were told at his funeral, that he was in Nigeria to meet with Bishops to discuss this very matter. An unfortunate incident occurred that was to end Titus's life, but we all know that his gentle spirit, his dream and vision will live on, fulfilled by those, whose dream it has now become!

Such is the Body of Christ, working together. As one party weakens, stronger parties take over, working for God and fulfilling each other's needs.

I once heard believers in Christ described as 'a coal fire'; all the parts burning happily together, but when one piece of coal falls out, the fire becomes smaller as the piece of fallen coal stops burning and loses power on its own.

We, as brothers and sisters need each other, each one has special gifts to build up the Body of Christ and if we play our part - what power we have united together.

How good and pleasant it is when brothers live together in unity.
(Psalm 133:1)

The Body of Christ

I am part of the Body of Christ
I feel it working well within
I stand receiving my gift of life
As God washes away all my sin.

There are many parts still to find
And yet, although few we stand
With open eyes - no longer blind
Together an eye, a foot, a hand.

We wait for others to come
Brand new refreshing parts
The old, the sick, the very young
Fitting around 'a loving heart'.

And when the Body of Christ
Is filled and quite complete
Like an engine purring with life
It will march on strengthened feet…

Towards God's promised land
With Jesus Christ at the head
Each child, each woman, each man,
With a loving message to spread.

And when the Body of Christ
Stands high upon holy ground
Filled with God's abundant life
God's purpose for us will be found.

If the whole body were an eye, where would the sense of hearing be? If the whole body were an ear, where would the sense of smell be? But in fact God has arranged the parts in the body, every one of them, as he wanted them to be.

(1 Corinthians 12:17-18)

Circles of Love

If you reach out to touch all the people you know
Giving them a little of God's pure love to grow
Sowing a seed inside each precious heart
Giving God's love a brand-new start
They in turn-will touch the people they know
And we will see God's love starting to grow
In small circles - creating more circles
Reaching everyone around the world
Each circle filled with God's purest love
And then,
The world WILL feel the presence of God.

Speaking the truth in love, we will in all things grow up into him who is the head, that is, Christ. From him the whole body, joined and held together by every supporting ligament, grows and builds itself up in love, as each part does it's work.

(Ephesians 4:15-16)

I can imagine these tiny circles increasing and I picture it in my mind, just like a cluster of frog spawn, each tiny circle filled with God's love but joined closely by others.

Often, we feel insignificant in this amazing world and that we have nothing special to offer. God created each one of us, counting the hairs on each head.

Indeed the very hairs of your head are all numbered. Don't be afraid you are worth more than many sparrows.
(Luke 12:7)

He chose us individually and just like a single grain of sand helping to make up a beach, without each Christian, there would be no Body of Christ.

RICHARD AND I were in Maidenhead one evening. As we walked, we saw a few pieces of jigsaw lying on the ground and I immediately thought of the Body of Christ and wrote the following:

Jigsaw

Tiny pieces of jigsaw
Scattered on the ground
Waiting for the day
When they would be found

No place to call their own
Until Jesus pays the cost
And gathers each one alone
To join others who were lost.

Differing shapes and sizes
Amazing colours and hues
Each one needed precisely
Each one like me and you.

Each piece so cleverly fashioned
And lovingly placed close by
Creating a beautiful pattern
As God plans each tiny life.

If there are pieces missing
Jesus will seek until He finds
Each precious piece of jigsaw
To make His picture so divine.

And when He has filled all the spaces
A beautiful picture will be seen
With colours to contrast and harmonise
God's picture of 'you' and 'me'.

Jesus the Head and the Bridegroom
The Body His beautiful bride
For whom He's prepared special rooms
For His children 'The Body of Christ'.

For you were like sheep going astray, but now you have returned to the shepherd and overseer of your souls.

(1 Peter 2:25)

I REMEMBER GIVING the next poem to Titus. He liked it. "It speaks to me," he said. "I will use it for the Christ's Family Church bulletin."

Brothers and Sisters

They gather all around me
Like the warming radiant sun
Blessing me and loving me
As though I am the only one
My brothers and my sisters
With their arms held wide
Shining with the love of Jesus
and sharing their precious lives
We each grow together
Our gifts and talents we share
Each precious sister and brother
Showing how much we care
We are the body chosen
With Jesus as the Head
We follow his paths closely
And safely we are led.

So in Christ we who are many form one body and each member belongs to all the others.
(Romans 12:5)

WHAT JOY I feel when I am with my brothers and sisters. Whatever their nationality, there is harmony. I feel the warming love of those around me. When Titus came to our home, or to our church, he always said, "I feel very comfortable amongst you all." Our backgrounds, culture and upbringing were alien and yet, we all experienced 'a bonding' between us.

Richard and I have learnt so much from our relationship with Ronke, Titus, and the girls, and their sisters and brothers within the Body of Christ. We have often discussed this. The Body of Christ does work, crossing all barriers and boundaries.

Sparkling Jewels

I see amongst my brothers and sisters
Jewels that sparkle in the noonday sun
Like glistening stars in the nighttime darkness
Like beacons shining in the raging storm.

To some they are a wonderful lifeline
To others they are the truest of friends
Always there in the sad and bad times
When we break-others are there to mend

Always a reliable shoulder to cry on
Always a sympathetic listening ear
Always there with two loving arms
Always there to care and share

Like diamonds! My brothers and sister
So many lights across the world
Sparkling with the pure love of Jesus
And filled with the radiance of God.

We have different gifts according to the grace given us.
(Romans 12:6)

ONE THING THAT impresses me is that whether homeless or wealthy, we are all equal in God's eyes. It has been a joy to meet such a variety of wonderful Christians, from so many walks of life, which otherwise, would have been denied us. Each Christian is a precious jewel.

Titus's dream was for an all-powerful worldwide Body of Christ, and I wrote the following poem to illustrate the power that Christians could have if they were united.

A Powerful Force

A tiny snowflake
Falls to the ground
Searching for its place
Joining others around.

A mound of snow
Transforming the scene
Is now so strong
It needs man's machine
To move 'this body'
Of flakes of snow
United together
And continuing to grow.

We in isolation
Are tiny flakes of snow
But bonded together
We powerfully grow.

The body is a unit though it is made up of many parts and though all its parts are many they form one body.
(1 Corinthians 12:12)

It is wonderful to see 'The Body' united, bonded and working together in love, each person playing his or her part!

Together In Love

Go quietly when you speak God's words
Sincerely tell what you have learned
Be open to God like a tiny child
Let God speak clearly into your mind
Love God-trust God -give Him your all
Be childlike-even though you are tall
Walk alongside others fulfilling their needs
Sisters - brothers and those bereaved
Others who struggle within their own lives
Because you are part of 'The Body of Christ'.

Now you are the body of Christ and each one of you is part of it.
(1 Corinthians 12:27)

AS WE WALK with Jesus within the Body of Christ, we are delighted to see 'new Christians' joining us and strengthening 'the Body'. This harvest comes from seeds sown long ago by other believers. What a joy to see the harvest! This prompted me to write the next poem.

Harvest Time

Crops are standing plump and ripe
Grown from seeds sown long ago
It's Harvest Time! An abundant time!
Crops will be gathered fully grown.

Seeds once sown by man and God
Bring people into our church
To question us with hearts of love
To explore our faith and learn.

And as we harvest from those seeds
We welcome each precious child
Into the midst of those who believe
And into the Body of Christ.

For we were all baptised by one spirit into one body, whether Jews or Greeks, slave or free and we were given the one spirit to drink.
(1 Corinthians 12:13)

Those of us who have been involved in the 'harvesting of crops will know that it is hard work. The work has to take place at just the right moment, too early and the fruit or grain is not ready, too late and the crop may be spoiled. The weather plays its part too. Rain can completely ruin an abundant crop. When we have harvested our crop, we need somewhere dry in the right environment so that it does not spoil or rot. A great deal of care has to be taken.

As children who are newly born into the Christian faith, come into the Body, it will be hard work with lots of doubts, fears and questions to be dealt with.

Timing is critical too, the right word at the wrong moment will not be received well, if the child is not ready. A wrong word at the wrong moment may result in a person's faith being destroyed. Having harvested, it is essential that the environment is loving and sensitive. I often think about the time when I first entered St. Michael's church, I was welcomed and nurtured by people following their own special path and yet they took much time to answer my innocent 'baby' questions. I was loved and cared for throughout. I did experience 'a wrong word' and it did rock and unsteady me for a while, but God brought me quickly back on track.

AS WE FOLLOW Jesus as part of 'the Body', we also lead others - Jesus the shepherd leading his sheep in one single line along the narrow path, towards green pastures.

In Faith We Walk

I reach out with my right hand
To the believer who will lead me
With confidence and knowledge
The Christian who will teach me.

I reach out with my left hand
To find a newly born child
To follow me across the land
As I become this person's guide.

And as each new day passes
I follow as I am led
Guided by my saviour Jesus
My master at the head.

He gathered me from a dusty road
And found me a special friend
Who guided me and took my load
And helped me to see ahead.

Joyfully we walk God's path
Laid especially for each of us
We walk in light through the dark
The Body moving in faith and trust.

Therefore, brothers, since we have confidence to enter the most holy place by the blood of Jesus by a new and living way opened for us through the curtain that is, His body.

(Hebrews 10:19-20)

The Body

I live within a circle
A circle with my friends
Who live closely by me
A circle that never ends.

I live within a circle
A circle filled with love
An invisible circle
Filled with the love of God.

I live within a circle
Of loving family friends
A worldwide family circle
'The Body' that has no end.

We are all members of one body.

(Ephesians 4:25)

I WAS ASTONISHED at the number of people I met at Titus's funeral who were determined to fulfil Titus's dream. I felt a renewed spirit there waiting to carry on his work.

I tell you the truth, unless a grain of wheat falls to the ground and dies, it remains only a single seed. But if it dies it produces many seeds.
(John 12:24)

Vision for Unity

This day was precious
We were sharing treasured moments
A beautiful flower had fallen
But the stem and buds were perfect
Waiting to grow into blossoms and bloom
And as we sung the last hymn
Tears fell gently from heaven
Accompanied by radiant sun
Suddenly God provided His sign
Not one but two rainbows appeared
And we knew that God was by our side
Supporting and watching His children
Understanding their loss and pain
We were all there sharing together
Sweet memories made on this day
Friends - family - sisters and brothers
Brought together by this loving man
We stood bonded in our love for him and God

Unity - unity the Body united on this day
And Bishop Titus David's dream was planted
His vision for unity was 'beginning to be.'

Make every effort to keep the unity of the spirit through the bond of peace. There is one body and one spirit.
(Ephesians 4:3-4)

Bishop Titus David lived his life loving God and Jesus, reflecting so many of God's characteristics and sharing with us the deep love that God and Jesus have for each one of us.

As a person he displayed all the fruits of the spirit and had many spiritual gifts which enabled him to carry out his varied and responsible duties throughout the world.

He was the founder of and Bishop to Christ's Family Church in London, UK, Lagos and Ibadan in Nigeria.

On Bishop Titus's 'handout' with his personal details, he said, "Please pray for me and pray for us too that God may open a door for our message, So that we may proclaim the mystery of Christ." (Colossians 4:3).

Bishop Titus was a family man who greatly valued and loved Ronke, his wife, and his three beautiful daughters, Melody, Rachael, and Damilola, wanting the very best for them.

When I was thinking about Poems For Titus and relating it to our Father God and Jesus His Son, I re-read the creation and thought about the amount of preparation and work that God put into this truly amazingly beautiful world, that He made for us, His children.

We see in Genesis the creation of both heaven and earth and step by step, the order in which God created the whole world, introducing every detail into His plan as it was carried out.

Man was not included until God had finished His work.

I find it very difficult to capture in words the immense character, creativity and amazing love of God and Jesus, SO I will follow this with a flavour of my OWN feelings in verse, towards this Almighty Power.

The Creator God

IN GENESIS WE read of the creation of heaven and earth and step by step we see 'the order' in which God created the world and the universe. Every tiny detail was carefully thought out and planned.

We are part of God's creation. He entrusted man to care for His creation, giving us rules to abide by, so that we could enjoy fellowship with Him and under His guidance live an abundant and fulfilling life.

When I look around me at the intricate detail that God has put into every tiny part of His creation, I am overwhelmed and truly amazed. Everything matters and has to be exactly right for Him, however small it is part of God's plan. And God's creation works, it is totally reliable. Whatever man does, God's world still functions as He has planned it to do.

Birds continue to nest, grass grows, the cycle of life continues. Throughout the Bible God teaches us His truths, His word and the true meaning of life.

For every animal is mine and the cattle
on a thousand hills. I know every bird in the
mountains and the creatures of the field are mine.
If I were hungry I would not tell you
for the world is mine and all that is in it.
(Psalm 50:10-12)

In the beginning God created the heavens and the earth. Now the earth was formless and empty, darkness was over the surface of the deep and the Spirit of God was hovering over the waters.

(Genesis 1:1-2)

Each Tiny Detail

Each...
A speck of dust
A grain of sand
A tiny pebble on a beach
A raindrop in a storm
Each one...
So tiny and insignificant in itself
And yet making up 'a whole'.

Without the grain of sand
Or the tiny pebble
There would be no beach.
Without the droplets of rain,
No rivers or seas.
However small
However tiny
It contributes to the whole.

Without each speck of dust
There would be no earth.
Without each leaf
There would be no trees

Without each tree,
No forest or shade.

Without each blade of grass
There would be no food
Each micro-organism is VITAL
TO THE WHOLE UNIVERSE
And each interdependent.

Mother earth providing
Stability and nourishment
And thus providing food
For all living creatures
Each part - however small
plays a VITAL role
Each whole-
Is dependent upon another 'whole'
And each whole playing its part in God's universe.

I will make your offspring like the dust of the earth so that, if anyone could count the dust, then your offspring would be counted.
(Genesis 13:16)

How important every minute insect or creature is to God and His "plan" , nothing is wasted.

Daily we see his tiny creatures 'tidying' up His world so that there is never a need for us to dust or polish. The natural world is kept beautifully spick and span by God's almighty plan.

God has surrounded us with beauty, variety and wonderment to be sure that we have absolutely everything we need.

The Lord has done great things for us and we are filled with joy.
(Psalm 126:3)

God Created Heaven and Earth

God creates each rainbow in the sky
So many flowers to please our eye
Mountains, valleys and running streams
Sandy beaches and salty seas
Colourful flowers that blossom and bloom
Filling each nostril with sweet perfume
Insects and beautiful birds on the wing
Waking us at dawn as they musically sing
The silvery moon and stars that shine
The warming sun - the day- the night
God created the heavens and the earth
And he made man to govern His world.

God saw all that He had made and it was very good and there was evening and there was morning - the sixth day.
(Genesis 1:31)

Father How?

Father how did you make the snowdrop so small
Peeping above the purest white snow
The honeysuckle and clematis against the wall
And the soft petals of the perfumed rose?

Father how did you make creatures that climb and crawl
The beautiful patterns of the butterflies' wings
Such wonderful coats to keep animals warm
Father how did you create everything?

How did you make the salty seas
The soothing breeze, the roaring wind
Tiny raindrops that plop onto leaves
And how did you teach each bird to sing?

Father how did you make the world
With mountains, valleys and beaches of sand
Seas that roar and water that swirls
And treasures placed underground for man?

Father how did you make all of us
Each one with a unique fingerprint
Differing faces - hair and noses
Assorted shapes and colour of skin?

So God created man in his own image.
In the image of God he created him.
Male and female he created them.
(Genesis 1:27)

I Think of God Everyday

I gaze up to the sky
At the rainbow So high
As clouds scurry by
And I think of God

I look at the trees
The design in each leaf
The rivers and streams
And I think of God

I gather flowers in bloom
To decorate my room
I enjoy their perfume
As my thoughts turn to God

I see creatures tiny and small
And animals large and tall
Some walk whilst others crawl
And I remember God

I listen to the birds
Making music to be heard
It's not too absurd
When I think of God

The snowflakes that fall
The effervescing waterfall
The rain against a wall
Makes me think of God

The detail in life
The stars shining bright
Perfection always right
Is why I think of God

It was not 'a big bang'
When life 'just began'
It was simply God's plan
For His universe and man.

And God said, "Let the land produce living creatures according to their kinds livestock, creatures that move along the ground and wild animals each according to its kind," and it was so.

(Genesis 1:24)

River Bank

The rushing water sparkles
Reflecting life close by
Free flowing it dances
Beneath a clear blue sky
Travelling from source to sea
Guided between firm banks
Ducks drift by with quacking beaks
Each creature's home the river bank.

Coots shriek in rhythmic beat
As land birds sing their song
A flock of flying honking geese
Show that their tunes too belong.
A nesting coot with twigs in beak
In this garden at river's edge
Intertwines each twig and leaf
Busying herself with woven nest.

The majestic willow's leaves
Reach gracefully down to touch
The cool clear water beneath
As raindrops fall from above
Creating new patterns to see
Upon the reflecting face
As creatures swim slowly at peace
Enjoying the river's space.

And God said, "Let the water teem with living creatures and let birds fly above the earth across the expanse of sky."

(Genesis 1:20)

Autumn In The Countryside

I love the countryside in autumn
As the leaves begin to change
Into colours soft and warm
Yellow - orange and red aflame.

Leaves gently flutter down
From the forest trees afire
Creating patterns on the ground
Blending colour with design

And as I walk through these leaves
They crunch beneath my feet
Like crispy crunchy cornflakes
Good enough to eat!

I give you every seed bearing plant on the face of the whole earth and every tree that has fruit with seed in it. They will be yours for food.

(Genesis 1:29)

And God said "Let the water under the sky be gathered to one place and let the ground appear" and it was so. God called the dry ground 'land' and the gathered waters he called 'seas' and God saw that it was good.

(Genesis 1:9-10)

The Seaside In Autumn

The autumn sun shines brightly
With a clear translucent light
Across the sea dancing lightly
With dazzling light so bright
The river swollen with rain
Rushes urgently passed
Pouring into pulsating waves
Creating patterns that dance
Splashing rushing whirlpools
Currents that swell with delight
Shimmering above the surface
Like diamonds So vividly bright
River meets sea with turbulence
And very soon they become one
Rhythmically moving together
Over sands beneath the sun
Sea birds wade in shallow waters
As beachcombers search beneath
The cliffs for tiny treasures
Brought in by the cleansing sea
The fiery setting sun dips
Mirrored by the water below
Across the seas shimmering surface
As cool sea breezes blow
There is just a hint of winter
As autumn leaves flutter down
As season follows season
And I enjoy the seaside sounds.

So God created the great creatures of the sea and every living and moving thing with which the water teems according to their kinds and every winged bird according to its kind and God saw that it was good.

(Genesis 1:21)

Wintertime

I love the season of wintertime
The air is fresh and clean
Fields are ploughed in line
In readiness to receive.

The dark rich soil is waiting
For new life from buried seeds
Overnight the countryside
Is kissed by frost in trees.

Glistening like starlight
As rabbits cosily sleep
Beneath the ground in daylight
While the foxes search and creep.

How clean the landscape
Looks after snowflakes fall
What fun making footprints
As snow drifts against the wall.

Clearly on the horizon
In bare winter coats
Trees stand like sculptures
Guarding the valleys below.

The countryside is bathed
In the purest golden light
Whilst all around is silent
A time of rest and quiet.

Waiting in expectation
Wintertime is at peace
Animals rest in hibernation
Secure in winter sleep.

By the seventh day God had finished the work he had been doing So on the seventh day he rested from all his work.

(Genesis 2:2)

And God said let there be lights in the expanse of sky to separate the day from the night and let them serve as signs to mark the seasons and days and years.

(Genesis 1:14)

Seasons Are Special

Springtime comes with bursting buds
The earth is cheered by sun that warms
In the darkest wood bluebells nod
And birds sing loud and clear at dawn
All around me buzzes with life
Bees are busy and hedgehogs wake
Frogs are croaking and birds swiftly fly
To and fro with new nests to make
Daffodils turn trumpets to the sky
Heady perfume scents the air
Branches are heavy with blossoms on high
The earth vibrates with life everywhere.

Summer follows on with ripening corn
Perfumed flowers and newly mown hay
Breezes ripple through the long grass
As animals rest in the heat of the day
The fruits of summer are everywhere
The sound of combines drone in the fields
Vegetables grow fast with plenty to share
Bees buzz happily collecting their yield
Mirrored dragonflies dart and dance
The air is warm, and the days are long
So that we can enjoy in abundance
All that summertime brings along.

Autumn comes with falling leaves
Yellow, gold, red and brown
Cold winds toss them from the trees
Bringing them gently to the ground
The fields are busy at harvest time
Gathering in the golden corn
Fruits and vegetables grown and ripe
Collected ready to preserve and store
The sky is filled with chasing clouds
Trees are adorned with frosty white
Birds are singing musical sounds
Cobwebs glisten as cold frost bites.

Winter's trees stand bare without leaves
Against a skyline of winter grey
Animals shelter amongst woodland trees
Long dark nights and the shortest days
Hedgehogs and rabbits are in sleep
Houses are lit and fires are ablaze
Bonfires are built high and neat
As children enjoy wintertime play
Fields are covered in winter white
Snowflakes settle on windowpanes
Houses sparkle with Christmas lights
As the postman delivers cards each day.

God made the wild animals according to their kinds. The livestock according to their kinds and all the creatures that move along the ground according to their kinds.

(Genesis 1:25)

Little Things

Don't you just love 'The Little Things'
A snowdrop peeping above the snow
Hearing the song as songbirds sing
Snowflakes fluttering as cool winds blow
Don't you just love 'The Little Things'
Waking early at the break of dawn
Observing the flight of geese on the wing
Watching still waters as raindrops fall.
Don't you just love 'The Little Things'
Seeing a rainbow appear in the sky
Hearing the sound as church bells ring
Sitting beside a blazing log fire.
Don't you just love 'The Little Things'
Enjoying God's creation every day
Following Jesus of your own free will
Reflecting on God and kneeling to pray.
Don't you just love 'God's Little Things'!

Whenever the rainbow appears in the clouds, I will see it and remember the everlasting covenant between God and all living creatures of every kind on earth.

(Genesis 9:16)

I OFTEN WONDER whether we would recognise God if He came to earth disguised as a man. I also wonder what His response would be as He investigated His creation closely and saw how man had altered it. Of course, God does know, He sees everything, but I had some fun writing this with "tongue in cheek"!

God Came To "Walk In The Garden"

God - He came down from heaven
To walk in the garden again
To observe His world - His creation
And to see what "Adam" had done.
At first, He stood on a mountain
Enjoying the wondrous scene
Then He walked through the heather
Making His way towards the sea.
He walked along the sandy beaches
Amongst plastic and discarded waste
He wiped tar from His feet
As He reminisced - remembering
What He'd placed in the sea.
He looked for the mammals and fish
Each one carefully designed by Him.
The water He'd made was crystal clear
And bore no resemblance to what was here

So…

God decided to leave at a fast pace
And no one on this beach knew Him.
He remembered a forest of trees nearby

He'd once filled it with wildlife and butterflies.
He walked briskly along a tarmac road
As cars sped passed Him brushing His clothes
And no one He saw on this road knew Him.
At last, He came to the site of the forest
Where the trees were - now stood houses,
Skyscraper flats and concrete blocks
And no one He saw there knew Him.

God's ears ached with the sound of the traffic
And fumes from exhausts filled His lungs.
He started to cough. But it was getting late
And God walked quickly on into the night
Music blasting from cars passing by
His eyes became dazzled by their lights
And He approached the town somewhat dazed
And no one He met in this town knew Him.
He saw people in the brightly lit restaurants
Laughing, eating and wearing smart clothes.
He saw outside on the pavements
the homeless and the poor that nobody owns.
At last, He found a beautiful building
"Somewhere quiet to rest" God thought.
He found seats where people were sitting
And discreetly He found a seat at the back.
He listened carefully - the vicar spoke of 'God'
And He enjoyed the music and all of the songs.
The service progressed and they spoke of 'love'
But no one in this church knew Him!

THE CREATOR GOD wants what is best for us in order that we may enjoy an abundant life in His wonderful world. We enjoy God's creation every day all around us, the beautiful ever-changing skies and the glorious array of colours. The moon and stars that fill my mind with wonderment. The changing seasons and all that those seasons have to offer us, in beauty, detail and design. The incredible assortment of creatures; animals, birds, insects, reptiles etc.

Amazing countries and people so different from our own, incredible scenery, mountains to climb, seas, rivers, streams etc.

When I walk in the countryside I am in awe of the beauty, the patchwork fields and the beautiful shapes and sculptures of the trees.

In springtime our garden is ablaze with blossoming trees, flowering shrubs and spring flowers carpeting the ground. Their perfume is intoxicating and what wonderful fruits and vegetables God has provided for our taste buds. Everything we need is provided in abundance.

Whilst we live out our daily lives on earth, God continues to surround us with His creativity and beauty.

Then God said, "Let the land produce vegetation seed bearing plants and trees on the land that bear fruit with seed in it according to their various kinds," and it was so.

(Genesis 1:11)

ON 27TH FEBRUARY 2002, the day of Bishop Titus's funeral, God's amazing creation was everywhere, flowers blooming, blossom filled trees in pink and white, filled gardens and parks, daffodils shone out from the ground, and I felt inspired to write the following:

Rainbows Met Daffodils

Daffodils were blooming
Beneath blossom filled trees
The day was dawning
And the skies were grey
I longed for a rainbow
To appear in the sky
So that we would know
That God was nearby.

The Body of Christ united that day
As they shared their special love
Friends and family - sang and prayed
For Bishop Titus Olugbenga David.

We were saying goodbye
to a very precious man
A dear friend - Bishop - brother
A shepherd with a guiding hand
And as memories were being made
We felt God's warming love
Gentle tears mingled with sun rays
Sorrow met with the glory of God

Radiance met with gentle showers
And God gave His children a sign
As rainbows met daffodils
And 'The Body' stood side by side.

Whenever I bring clouds over the earth and the rainbow appears in the clouds I will remember my covenant between me and you and all living creatures of every kind.
(Genesis 9:14-15)

God lovingly planned the world so carefully. He chose us and loves us along with all of His creation. Despite our sins His ultimate wish for us, is that we should love the Lord our God with all our hearts, so intensely, that there is no separation, God living within each one of us as we live within Him.

He commands us to love our neighbour as ourselves and if only we were able to do this, we would never hurt or injure another person again, in thought, word or deed, because of our love for God and our neighbour.

Thinking about God's will and love for us all, I will conclude with my favourite words from Isaiah.

The wolf will live with the lamb,
the leopard will lie down with the goat.
the calf and the lion and yearling together;
and a little child will lead them.
The cow will feed with the bear,
their young will lie down together,
and the lion will eat straw like the ox.
The infant will play near the hole of the cobra,
and the young child put his hand into the viper's nest
They will neither harm nor destroy
on all my holy mountain,
for the earth will be full of the knowledge of the LORD
as the waters cover the sea.

(Isaiah 11:6-9)

God Is Love

Whoever lives in love
lives in God and God in him
(1 John 4:16)

WHEN I REMEMBER Titus, I recall his beaming smile and especially his sparkling eyes as he praised God in song.

He was a man of God, whose generous love was returned to him; just as he loved everyone, so everyone who met Titus loved him in return. His gentle loving spirit was filled with God's love. When we were with him, we could feel his love.

A Loving Spirit

A loving face beaming with life
Two loving eyes sparkling with light
A welcoming smile from lips that grin
A loving voice to beautifully sing
Two loving arms to warmly hug
A glowing face that shines with love.

God's comforting love surrounds us here on earth. He so loves each one of us that he gave His only son, Jesus to die on the cross for the forgiveness of our sins. Such was His great love.

Love is patient, love is kind. It does not envy, it does not boast, it is not proud. It is not rude; it is not self-seeking. It is not easily angered and keeps no records of wrongs.

(1 Corinthians 13:4-5)

God's Crown of Love

There is no love greater
Than that of our loving God
Who gave His son as Saviour
Willingly to show His love.

Towards His wayward children
Giving special gifts from above
To each precious child 'a jewel'
In God's crown of love.

For God so loved the world that he gave his one and only son, that whoever believes in him shall not perish but have eternal life.

(John 3:16)

God's Love

I feel Your love surging into my mind
It warms me - filling me from head to toe
Giving me new energy and a renewed life
Penetrating deeply into my soul.
I feel it saturating my whole being
Permeating into every muscle throughout
Flowing into every blood vessel and capillary
Filling my deeply aching heart
Breathing fresh breath into my lungs
Until my whole being is drenched
Soaked - saturated with Your perfect love
And I feel alive with renewed strength.

*Whoever believes in me as the scripture has said,
streams of living water will flow from within him.*
(John 7:38)

Whatever we do in life, however far we stray, God is always there to forgive, help and restore us.

I REMEMBER CLEARLY a wonderful vivid dream I once had. In the dream I was a little girl walking a beautiful path with a very large man. There were times when I wanted to explore at the side of the path, or further afield. This man just sat patiently on a nearby rock, waiting for me to come back. In this dream I felt secure and loved and this beautiful path brought me back to him. He would stand up taking my hand once again and we would walk together a little further, until I was ready to explore again. He was such a patient loving person and when I recall this dream, it brings tears to my eyes.

I believe that the man in the dream represented God and the dream was showing God's love for me; His kindness and patience waiting for me to return whenever I strayed from Him. The dream prompted me to write:

God's Amazing Love

However far we stray
From God's own path
However long before
We return - as we are.

God is always waiting
With arms open wide
His heart brimming
With deep love inside.

However far we have walked
Whatever we have done
God is there to support
With his amazing love.

And you also were included in Christ when you heard the word of truth, the Gospel of your salvation. Having believed, you were marked in him with a seal, the promised Holy Spirit.

(Ephesians 1:13)

God's love is pure, perfect and unconditional, and have chosen us, you and me, He is willing to shower us and bless with this warming enveloping love.

God's abiding Love

God's love is the glue that bonds us
Holding us tightly until the storm subsides.
God's love is the brightest beacon
That shines on the darkest night.
God's love is the warmest sunshine
Lifting our hearts on a cold winter's day.
God's love is the refreshing raindrops
That sparkle and wash all the dust away.
God's love is the blossom in springtime
Filling the air with sweet perfume.
God's love is the melody from songbirds
That wakes us at the break of dawn.

Be imitators of God therefore as dearly loved children an live a life of love.

(Ephesians 5:1)

GOD'S LOVE SURROUNDS us everywhere but unless man recognises this love, he will not be able to benefit from it. God, forever faithful and loving, continues to sow His seeds of love around us until they take root and grow in our hearts.

Then we will no longer be infants, tossed back and forth by the waves and blown here and there by every wind of teaching and by the cunning and craftiness of men in their deceitful scheming.
(Ephesians 4:14)

God's Seeds of Love

A fragile seed of love
So tiny - so vulnerable
Bursting with energy and life
It's home - a tiny crack
In the fragile pavement of life
Where men follow like sheep
Their latest fads that will fade
Like the rainbows they chase
In their search for freedom
And yet freedom does not lie
At the end of this road
Each paving slab laid by man
Human promises and manmade dreams.

One by one they fall
Into man-made traps
Imprisoned and ensnared

By their own choices in life
Building man laid paths
They become their own victims.

God's seed grows against all odds
Trampled by the feet of those
Who do not see or understand
The 'simplicity' and 'beauty'
Each one of its flowers - a gift
A blossom of love - perfect love
Trying to restore harmony
Creating fruits ready to feed
Nourish - guide - care for and teach
Some fruits will produce seeds
And if allowed to flourish and grow
Will ignite the hearts of man
Who will learn the secret
THE SECRET OF GOD'S FREEDOM
In a world that is blind
Blind to THE GLORY OF GOD
And to God's unconditional love.

God is light, in him there is no darkness at all.
(1 john 1:5)

Glimpses of Heaven

I see God's radiant light
Growing inside each loving heart
Deeply loving and shining bright
Warmly caring and responding to God
Like mirrors reflecting
God's powerful golden light
Tiny lights searching
Like beacons through the night
Finally connecting
Through prayer - each child of God
Requesting - communicating
With their Father God in love.

Love and faithfulness meet together, righteousness and peace kiss each other, faithfulness springs forth from the earth and righteousness looks down from heaven.

(Psalm 85:10-11)

God's Flowers

Flowers grown in God's garden
Given to us with His love
From His own seeds of truth
Precious blossoms grown by God
Showing His faithful devotion
Given with His deepest love
Chosen for us - His children
Flowers filled with His love.

How great is the love the Father has lavished on us, that we should be called children of God and that is what we are.
(1 John 3:1)

Pure Gold

Pure gold flowing from the hand of God
Tumbling rushing like a mountain stream
Dancing with life and sparkling with love
Reaching us joyfully to cleanse and clean.

The purest gold like the rising dawn
Refreshing and renewing each broken part
Like a fresh day in early morn
Giving us all a brand-new start.

The very best - the finest gold
So warming and comforting like the setting sun
Generously given by the Creator God
Who willingly gave His own precious Son.

Golden gifts from a loving God
To a world filled with darkness and pain
Understanding and healing with amazing love
And forgiving us with mercy and grace.

Gold continually pouring from the heart of God
Even though man has disobeyed
He still gives us His unending love
And He's still there when we seek His face.

Then the angel showed me the river of the water of life, as clear as crystal, flowing from the throne of God and of the lamb down the middle of the great city. On each side of the river stood the tree of life, bearing twelve crops of fruit, yielding its fruit every month. And the leaves of the tree are for healing the nations.

(Revelation 22:1-2)

GOD IS SO generous to us in this "fallen' world. He loves us and cares about us all and wants the best for us. He loves us unconditionally.

I have been given SO much by God's mercy and grace. My life has been transformed by His great love for me.

God's Great Love

I find comfort in the arms of God
Peace from the loving heart of God
Joy in the knowledge of God
And wisdom from the mind of God.

I see beauty through the eyes of God
I hear music through the ears of God
I feel gentleness from the touch of God
I breathe the life force from the breath of God.

I find shelter in the house of God
Forgiveness by the grace of God
Security as I walk closely to God
And protection beneath the wings of God

I find fellowship in the family of God
I feel purpose in my life with God
I found my Saviour in the Son of God
And eternal life - a gift from God.

IN THIS WORLD where good and evil walk side by side, God's children will find it tough at times, but God is there catching us when we fall, comforting us, drying our tears, healing our wounds and strengthening us from the inside, His light always shining brightly for all His children.

God's Faithful Love

When the storm rages like a tempest
And the paths are steep and rough
When you feel alone and empty
God will fill you with His love.

When the rivers flow like torrents
And the earth quakes beneath your feet
Then Jesus is there beside you
With His joy and loving peace.

When the mountain is too high
And you feel you have no breath
Jesus's arms will open wide
And He'll find you easy steps.

When your boat becomes unsteady
And you fear it will subside
Jesus will be the lighthouse ready
To beam out its golden light.

And hope does not disappoint us because God has poured out his love into our hearts by the Holy Spirit whom he has given us.
(Romans 5:5)

HOW REFRESHING IT is in summer to walk along the beach with the soft damp sand squeezing between your toes, enjoying the refreshing salt sprays and the summer breezes, as the rhythmic sea gently washes the shore.

On a beautiful summer's day, I remember gazing out to sea, watching the sun glistening like diamonds on the sea's surface and this inspired me to write:

Gifts So Pure

Tumbling sparkling - refreshing - cooling
Rhythmically moving like the waves of the sea
Dancing in pure light - invigorating renewing
Filled with energy - so vital - so clean
Coming to us from the centre of God
Flowing freely into each heart with life
A gift so pure in light and love
Refreshing the hearts of each chosen child
God's gifts given with His great love
Straight from the heart of the Creator Divine
Gifts so pure from our Father God
And His son Jesus who gave us His life.

Every good and perfect gift is from above, coming down from the Father of heavenly lights who does not change like shifting sands.
(James 1:17)

Unlike us, God knows no boundaries. He loves us all unconditionally.

Remember those in prison as if you were their fellow prisoners and those who are ill-treated as if you yourselves were suffering.
(Hebrews 13:3)

Love For All

God's love is for the sick - the poor
His love is for those who are at war
Jesus loves the weak and abused
The drunkard and the wrongly accused
God loves the father - the mother - the child
And each one of us - however wild!
We are nothing without God's love
Given freely - this love from God.

God's Precious Gift

I shall always treasure
God's wonderful gift of love
That comes from our Heavenly Father
His special gift for us
God alone will give it
Through Jesus Christ His Son
God's precious gift of perfect love
Given freely to each one.

Praise be to the God and Father of our Lord Jesus Christ, who has blessed us in the heavenly realms with every spiritual blessing in Christ.

(Ephesians 1:3)

GOD HAS LAID a beautiful path for each one of us with 'special goals' and achievements for Us to find and with this in mind I wrote:

Exquisite Path

Exquisite path
Of purest gold
Scattered jewels
As life unfolds
Born out of love
For earthly child
Each fibre spun
By God's great hand

A golden path
Of wisdom and truth
A golden path
That leads us through
A golden path
Of peace and love
A golden path
Laid for us by God.

You have made known to me the path of life.
(Psalm 16:11)

For he chose us in him before the creation of the world to be holy and blameless in his sight. In love he predestined us to be adopted as his sons through Jesus Christ in accordance with his pleasure and will.

(Ephesians 1:4-5)

God's Dreams

God has laid a beautiful path
Each pavier is a 'gift' for us
To enable us to find God's heart
And to receive His grace and trust.

Be careful how you walk God's path
Each part laid with His sweet love
Made from His forgiving heart
Don't trample down God's dreams for us!

Let us then approach the throne of grace with confidence in so that we may receive mercy and find grace to help us our time of need.

(Hebrews 4:16)

I am the gate, whoever enters through me will be saved.

(John 10:9)

A Chosen Path

We each have a chosen path to walk
A path that leads to an eternal life
Our path is laid, and we can choose
To walk or leave this path of light,
To search blindly for those golden gates
Or to walk this special path with God
To follow His radiant golden light
Believing - trusting and walking in love
Accepting His words believing His truths
And walking this chosen path with God.

In him we have redemption through his blood, for the forgiveness of sins in accordance with the riches of God's grace that he lavished on us with all wisdom and understanding.

(Ephesians 1:7-8)

SOMETIMES WE 'TRAP' ourselves and bind ourselves with all sorts, 'baggage' that we carry with us from our past. Fears that we still retain from life's experiences, but God can take all our 'baggage' away and give us a fresh new life to enjoy with Him.

A New Circle

I once made a circle
It went all around me
I lived inside this circle
Away from the world to see
But God came into my circle
And the circle He uncurled
Taking me out by the hand
And showing me His world.

God made me a new circle
And He made it with His arms
Enclosing me and protecting me
And keeping me from harm
Lovingly He nurtured me
And became my special guide
Giving me new eyes to see
And a brand-new life!

God has given us eternal life and this life is in his son.
(John 5:11)

JUST AS A parent feels the pain of his or her child, so it is with God. I believe, He suffers with us - our pain and sadness and this prompted me to write:

Holy Spirit

God stands amongst His children
Although invisible to human eye
He too suffers with them
God who breathes in life
And although man deceives
God brings us His light
Through the Holy Spirit's peace
And with gifts and love divine
His Spirit! "A cool clear stream"
That refreshes our aching hearts
His Spirit! - "A fire aflame"
That ignites every part
His Spirit! - "A mighty wind"
Cleansing our sins away
God's Spirit - is amazingly alive
And lives with us each day.

May the grace of the Lord Jesus Christ and the love of God and the fellowship of the Holy Spirit be with you all.
(2 Corinthians 13:14)

Father God

TITUS LOVED OUR Father God and I remember him once saying to me, "Everything I have belongs to God". Titus was fatherly too and had a deep love for those around him. He loved and genuinely cared for everyone. Titus made each one of us feel special, praying for us individually and loving us with a father' s heart. He gave freely of himself and his time, cheerfully giving to God's work and wanting the very best for us all; nothing was too much trouble for him. After the tragic accident, I realised that Titus had given so many sweet memories for us all to reflect upon and this inspired me to write:

Sweet Memories

Bishop David once said of himself
That he was made in heaven
To be born on earth
With family, brothers, sisters, friends
Making with each one 'sweet memories'
Now to treasure and reflect upon
And with love we remember these
So many individual memories
His loving ways - his radiant smile
His grace, humour and humility
His vision for the world and zest for life
But most of all his father's heart
Welcoming, sharing, nurturing, feeding
So many fruits - so many gifts
Teaching, listening, shepherding, caring
Overcoming fear and prejudice

Bishop David so generously shared
And gave out his abundant love
Loving others as he loved himself
Sharing the word and truths from God.

As for Titus, he is my partner and fellow - worker among you.
(2 Corinthians 8:23)

WHEN I THINK about our Father in Heaven, I find it astonishing that this incredible power of love knew me before I was born!

O Lord you have searched me and know me.
(Psalm 139:1)

My Father God

God tells me that He knew me
Long before I was born
He is always there beside me
Even when I was being formed
God waits for me to open the door
The choice is mine to make
He reaches down with gifts so pure
For me to seek and take
God surrounds me with His angels
Watching over me through the night
He is my Master and Servant humble
My Saviour, my Father, my Guide.

For you created my inmost being you knit me together in my mother's womb.
(Psalm 138:13)

GOD ESTABLISHED THE world for man and as a loving Father He has the best plans for us, to grow spiritually. We can choose our own path. He allows us to do that, always carefully watching. When we do cry out to Him, He is there to help us if we ask.

Ask and it will be given to you, seek and you will find, knock and the door will be opened to you.
(Matthew 7:7)

Life's Picture

When we are born
God lays at our feet
A picture to form
A story to complete
A pathway to find
A journey to travel
It is 'our' story of life
For us to unravel.
There are others to share
Our journey through life
As we seek here and there
In happiness or strife
We learn as we go
As new ventures appear
A family to love
And friends to hold dear
And as we reach the end
Of our journey through life
We reflect on 'our picture'
Almost complete in our sight.

The Lord is my light and my salvation whom shall I fear? The Lord is the stronghold of my life of whom shall I be afraid?

(Psalm 27:1)

God gives us everything that we need spiritually.

How precious to me are your thoughts O God - how vast is the sum of them. If I were to count them they would outnumber the grains of sand.

(Psalm 139:17-18)

God's Food

From God's own lips
Fall beautiful words
His word His truths
Our spiritual food
Words of love
To nourish my soul
Words of peace
To fill my mind
Words of joy
To heal my heart.

By day the Lord directs His love.
At night His song is with me.

(Psalm 42:8)

Gods Voice

God's voice is not like thunder
It is not as loud as a train
It does not sound like a trumpet
Or like an aeroplane.
God's voice is a gentle whisper
That speaks into my mind
And if I do not listen
I will miss His words Divine.

*Your word is a lamp to my feet
and a light for my path.*
(Psalm 119:105)

God created beautiful sounds for us to listen to. In nature, the whistling wind, breezes, fluttering leaves, the roaring sea, waves pounding against rocks or on beaches. The incredibly varied sounds from animals, birds and insects.

God has given us a variety of musical instruments and beautiful singing voices to enjoy.

*He put a new song in my mouth
a hymn of praise to God.*
(Psalm 40:3)

God's Music

Symphonies and orchestras
Sweet music to each ear
Dancing feet to rhythmic beat
As music fills the air
Sweet bird song from tiny throats
Such variety everywhere
Choirs singing in unison
Harmonies to enjoy and hear.

You will go out in joy and be led forth in peace. The mountains and hills will burst into song before you and all the trees of the field will clap their hands.
(Isaiah 55:12)

God is light in Him there is no darkness at all.
(1 John 1:5)

The Lord gives sight to the blind. The Lord lifts up those who are bowed down.
(Psalm 46:8)

She Now Saw

She was young
With perfect sight
Her eyes were good
By day and night
She had perfect vision
And could see afar

And yet...

She had not seen
The beauty of God's world.

She walked under a tree
Afire with autumn colour
She did not notice
The perfume of the rose
She did not see
The setting sun
She did not rise
To see a new day dawn

Until one day...

God spoke to her
And she cried out with joy
When she looked - she saw
God's world of beauty.
It had always been there
But despite her perfect vision
She had not seen
What SHE NOW SAW!

If I rise on the wings of dawn, if I settle on the far side of the sea, even there your hand will guide me, your right hand will hold me fast.

(Psalm 139:9-10)

GOD GIVES US His light to guide us through this world.

Let us walk in the light of the Lord.
(Isaiah 2:5)

God's Light

Each chosen child with shining light
Twinkling like the stars above
Journeying through earthly life
Searching - seeking - reflecting God.

God's radiant enveloping light
Overseeing, nurturing
As they twinkle and they shine
Communicating - Questioning

God blesses their every prayer
Each child speaking to Father God
Knowing that He's always there
Linked by light enfolded by love.

The sun will no more be your light by day nor will the brightness of the moon shine on you for the Lord will be your everlasting light and your God will be your glory.
(Isaiah 60:19)

I WAS BROUGHT up in a Christian home as a Christian child, attending Sunday School and church each Sunday. However, when I was seventeen years of age, we moved house and although we joined the local church, there was no one of my age there and I lost interest in church life.

I have strayed like a lost sheep.
(Psalm 119:176)

We were married in church and always spoke of joining church, but somehow it didn't happen. After a very long illness, I cried out to God and He answered that prayer.

I call on the Lord in my distress and he answers me.
(Psalm 120:1)

He told me clearly of His existence in a way that I could understand. He has taken care of me ever since and my life has totally changed.

I waited patiently for the Lord He turned to me and heard my cry. He lifted me out of the slimy pit out of the mud and mire. He set my feet on a rock and gave me a firm place to stand.
(Psalm 40:1-2)

We love because he first loved us.
(1 John 4:19)

My immediate reaction on finding God, was, "What a waste my life has been," and thinking of all those wasted years I wrote:

All Those Years

I lived all those years not knowing You
And now You are part of me
I do not know what I would do
If You were not here with me.
You are my precious Father God
You are my Loving Saviour
I lived all those years not knowing You
And now You are part of me.

If anyone obeys his word, God's love is truly made complete in him. This is how we know we are in him.
(1 John 2:5)

Having found God, I was like the Prodigal Son as described in Luke 15:11-31 and I was filled to overflowing with God's true love.

As the deer pants for streams of water so my soul pants for you o God.
(Psalm 42:1)

I just wanted to tell everyone about God, but I met with some rather disbelieving souls and this prompted me to write:

They Cannot See

I feel the warmth of God's own love
Such excitement - I feel I will burst
With God's joy from heaven above
And small miracles as I learn
I long to share with those I know

BUT...

They look blankly back at me
Because their eyes are tightly closed
They cannot see what I now see
They do not know what I now know.

The spirit of truth. The world cannot accept him, because it neither sees him nor knows him. But you know him, for he lives with you and will be in you.
(John 14:17)

WE CAN ALL be comforted by the knowledge that our Father God watches over us, blessing us and loving us and there is a very special feeling when we are very closely united with our Father in heaven.

My Father's Love

I love that wonderful warm feeling
That I know can only come from God
As He bathes me in His heavenly light
Refreshing me with energy and life
I feel relaxed - cosy and secure
Knowing God's purest perfect love
Resting in His comforting arms
And knowing Him as my Father God.

Though you have not seen him you love him and even though you do not see him now, you believe in him and are filled with inexpressible and glorious joy.
(1 Peter 1:8)

The Light of God

I see the shadow
The dark dark shadow
As it creeps across the world
Trying to extinguish the light.
But the light of God
Is constant - brightly shining
Protecting - teaching - leading
Lovingly watching, never dimming
Always encouraging and guiding
And as these tiny lights shine
From each one of His children
Reflecting His light back to Him
Sparkling with His peace, joy and love
Father and Son unite - they are one.

See darkness covers the earth and thick darkness over the peoples; but the Lord rises upon you and his glory appears over you.
(Isaiah 60:2)

Jesus, God's Son

TITUS LOVED JESUS and everything that He stood for. Jesus came into this world to fulfil God's will; He knew why and what lay before Him and yet because of His truly amazing love, He still came to die on the cross for each one of us. The life of Jesus is still an incredible story of obedience, humility and unconditional love.

The angel went to her and said, "Greetings you who are highly favoured. The Lord is with you."
(Luke 1:28)

A Tiny Babe

Jesus was predicted
When an angel came one day
Mary was scared and frightened
The angel said, "Don't be afraid"

And so...

On that very special day
In a humble home, a stable
A child - a vulnerable tiny babe
Was born to save His people.

She gave birth to her firstborn, a son. She wrapped him in cloths and placed him in a manger, because there was no room for them in the inn.
(Luke 2:7)

JESUS LOVED US so much that He was prepared to die for us, to take the burden of our sins, and to feel the separation from His Father God whom He loved. He wanted to teach us and show us that there is more to life than just living on earth. He wanted to show us through the resurrection that there is eternal life.

For this reason he had to be made like his brothers in every way, in order that he might become a merciful and faithful high priest in service to God, and that he might make atonement for the sins of the people.
(Hebrews 2:17)

I love the ant story which someone kindly told me when I was 'baby' Christian, and it helped me a great deal to understand why Jesus came down to earth to show us the way. For those who haven't heard it - I will tell it now. I do not know the author, but it is a good story!

If you wanted to divert some ants who were heading, one by one, following each other to a certain death, how would you do it?

It would be impossible to scoop them all up because they would run everywhere to get away.

If you put a large boulder in their path, they would walk over it.

If you put water in front of them, they would find a way around it.

If you were able to be born as an ant, you could show

the ants which path to take safely and they could, if they believed you, follow and you could teach, guide and lead them through safely.

This is precisely what Jesus did for us, He was born as one of us, He grew and lived as we do. He tried His best to divert us from the path that would result in certain death, to the path of light that leads to eternal life!

Since the children have flesh and blood he too shared in their humanity so that by his death he might destroy him who holds the power of death - that is the devil.

(Hebrews 2:14)

We can choose whether to believe Him, trust Him, and follow Him. It is our choice!

When God brings his firstborn into the world he says, "Let all God's angels worship him."

(Hebrews 1:6)

Vulnerable

How vulnerable the tiny seed
Soft and tender amongst choking weeds
How vulnerable the tiny flame
Trying to set alight the world.

How vulnerable was Jesus Christ
Who came to give each person life
Who through His unconditional love
Sacrificed and shed His own blood.

The word became flesh and made his dwelling among us. We have seen his glory, the glory of the One and Only, who came from the Father, full of grace and truth.
(John 1:4)

He is the image of the invisible God, the firstborn over all creation. For by him all things were created, things in heaven and on earth, visible and invisible, whether thrones or powers or rulers or authorities, all things were created by him and for him.
(Colossians 1:15-16)

How Can We Ignore Him

How can we ignore Him
When Jesus chose to come
To live here amongst us
Jesus - God's own son
He chose to guide us
And to be our friend
He came to teach us
To love and not fear death.

How can we ignore Him
When He gave up His life
Knowing what was before Him
Bringing us His purest light.
How can we ignore Him
The Creator of this world
How can we disbelieve Him
Or His beauty on this earth.

No-one has ever seen God, but God the One and Only who is at the Father's side, has made him known.

(John 1:18)

Jesus is always there for us.

For I am convinced that neither death nor life, neither angels nor demons, neither the present nor the future, nor any powers, neither height nor depth, nor anything else in creation will be able to separate us from the love of God that is in Christ Jesus our Lord.

(Romans 8:38-39)

Seed of Love

Jesus reaches down from heaven
With a tiny seed of love
He knows exactly where it is needed
This precious seed from God
If we accept this wonderful seed
And allow it to root on our hearts
Then we will begin to clearly see
And to experience 'a brand-new start.'

For you have been born again, not of perishable seed, but of imperishable, through the living and enduring word of God.

(1 Peter 1:23)

JESUS CARES FOR us like a loving father with his child, but it takes time for us to adapt to life as a child of God and this thought prompted me to write:

Two Hearts

Two hearts beat rhythmically
The old heart and the brand new one
The old heart deceiving
Whilst the new one loves
The old heart still sinning
Whilst the 'new' carries the blood
Of Jesus - refreshing - renewing
Filled with Peace, Joy, and Love
Until the old heart dies
And the new heart is the only one.

Create in me a pure heart O God and renew a steadfast spirit within me.
(Psalm 51:10)

JESUS ACCEPTS WHERE we are in life and cares for us until we are strong enough to follow His lead.

You should not be surprised at my saying, "You must be born again."
(John 3:7)

Born again

Jesus took my hand
So lovingly into His
Calling me "His child"
Accepting the way I live.
Filling my empty heart
With His precious love
Wiping away my tears
Telling me of His Father God.
Guiding me and loving me
Cradling me in His arms
Protecting and nurturing me
Shielding me from harm
Encouraging me to follow Him
Along the narrow pathway
Taking the burden of my sins
On this my special birthday.

In reply Jesus declared, "I tell you the truth no one can enter the kingdom of God unless he is born again of water and the spirit."
(John 3:5)

JESUS OUR LOVING Shepherd knows each one of us by name and takes care of us.

Take His Hand

Seek the hand of Jesus
As you trip or fall
Take hold of the hand of Jesus
As you hear His loving call
Take tightly the hand of Jesus
As you leave the familiar road
Take firmly the hand of Jesus
As He takes your heavy load
Hold onto the hand of Jesus
As you walk the narrow path
Trust in the hand of Jesus
As nightfall brings the dark.
Nestle into the hand of Jesus
As springtime bursts anew
Relax in the hand of Jesus
As summer brings perfume
Feel the warm hand of Jesus
In autumn's harvest time
Grip tightly to the hand of Jesus
As cold winter nips and bites
Trust in the hand of Jesus
He will lead you through
There is hope in the hand of Jesus
And His love is there for you.

The path of the righteous is level; O upright One, you make the way of the righteous smooth.
(Isaiah 26:7)

I once had a beautiful dream and wrote this poem about it.

My Dream

I saw once in a dream
The name "JESUS" across the sky
Lit by radiant sunbeams
It sparkled up on high.

Diamonds glistening in the sunlight
Telling the world His name
Jesus who came with life
A name above all names.

I saw banners waving
Reaching from earth to sky
Worshipping
Celebrating
Praising
Our Saviour's name so bright!

Therefore God exalted him to the highest place and gave him the name that is above every name.
(Philippians 2:9)

I REMEMBER LISTENING to a speaker, a missionary. She told us that she was once touched by a young man who said to her, "Would you please tell me about Jesus". I was touched too, so I wrote the following:

Please

Please tell me about Jesus
I really need to know
I had never heard of Jesus
Until the day you spoke.

Who told you about Jesus?
If they hadn't told you,
You wouldn't have known
And you couldn't tell me
About Jesus Christ
Then I would never have known!

For through him we both have access to the Father by one spirit.
(Ephesians 2:18)

I CANNOT REMEMBER who first told me about Jesus, at school, Sunday school, or my mother maybe, but I am forever grateful. Where would I be now, I wonder, without this wonderful person in my life?

It is for freedom that Christ has set us free. Stand firm then, and do not be burdened again by a yoke of slavery.
(Galatians 5:1)

My Friend

I look to my friend
For comfort and sharing
I look to my friend
For wisdom and caring
I look to my friend
To hold my hand tight
When I am afraid
Of the darkest night

I look to my friend
For His breathtaking smile
I look to my friend
As we walk the long mile
I look to my friend
For His guiding light
To protect me and guide me
My friend JESUS CHRIST!

I sought the Lord and he answered me. He delivered me from all my fears.

(Psalm 34:4)

How patient and kind Jesus is. I wonder how long He stands at the door waiting for us to open it?

Here I am I stand at the door and knock. If anyone hears my voice and opens the door I will come in and eat with him and he with me.

(Revelation 3:20)

Faith

Love came to visit me
I felt the warm embrace
But I turned away instantly
Until there was no trace.

Faith came along and spoke to me
I listened for a while
But I was blind and could not see
Faith's joyful radiant smile.

Some time now passed - I longed for love
But could not find love that day
Until I prayed and asked for God
To help me find the way.
Love and faith came into my life

Jesus, God's Son

And they each took a hand
And when I looked with 'open eyes'
It was Jesus holding my hands.

Jesus answered, "I am the way and the truth and the life. No-one comes to the Father except through me."
(John 14:6)

Jesus, Shepherd, Father, Saviour, Son of God and yet:

Jesus will lead ME

He's my father - I'm His child
He will protect ME
Like a hen with her brood
Jesus will lead ME
All I have to do is trust
And reach out for His hand
And let Him take mine in love.
To Him I'm just a child
Although I feel fully grown
He is there all the while
He is wise and TRULY KNOWS.

He will cover you with his feathers and under his wings you will find refuge. His faithfulness will be your shield and rampart.
(Psalm 91:4)

JESUS ACCEPTS US where we are and however broken we may be, He opens His loving arms and heart to us, bathing us in His healing love.

The Broken Pot

Jesus sees the beauty
In the broken pot
Thrown upon the rubbish heap
And left to fade and rot.

Others walk on by
Ignoring the broken heart
Not seeing with 'open eyes'
Every precious part.

But Jesus knows the potential
As He mends each tiny part
Until the pot is whole again
And can begin a brand-new start.

For he has rescued us from the dominion of darkness and brought us into the kingdom of the son he loves.
(Colossians 1:13-14)

Knowing Jesus

Knowing Jesus is better than
Seeing the brightest twinkling star
Watching the radiant setting sun
And the moon shining out afar.

Knowing Jesus is better than
The coolest breeze on the hottest day
Walking through fields of golden corn
And the scent of newly mown hay.

Knowing Jesus is better than
The most stunning rainbow overhead
Spectacular views from the mountain
And the aroma of freshly baked bread.

Knowing Jesus is better than
Making footprints in untrodden snow
Watching flames flicker and dance
Amongst the logs burning warm and slow.

Knowing Jesus is better than
The sweetest words and melodies
The most loving thought you've ever had
And loving arms to hold you near.

Knowing Jesus is better than
The most exquisitely perfumed rose
Holding a baby newly born
And watching this baby develop and grow.

Knowing Jesus is better than
Anything that brings me delight
Jesus a friend to every man
Who loved me enough to give His life.

Sweet Jesus

I see you in the morning mist
And when the sun goes down
I see you in the dew's soft kiss
Sparkling at the break of dawn.

I see you in each flake of snow
That flutters against the windowpane
I see you when the cool winds blow
And at the softest end of the day.

I see you in the crispest frost
That glistens in the bright sunshine
I see you in the softest moss
As I walk the many paths of life.

I see you in the radiance
And the rainbow crossing the sky
I see you in the refreshing rain
And in the warm breeze on high.

I see you in the raging seas
That thunder upon the softest sand
I see you in the crystal stream
That flows through narrow banks.

I see you in the sun's golden light
As it warms the soft brown earth
I see you in each star so bright
As it shines above this world.

I see you everywhere sweet Lord
In your gifts for each chosen child
I see you in your loving word
And in your ever guiding light.

The Lord has done great things for us and we are filled with joy.
(Psalm 126:3)

Jesus

Jesus has two strong arms
To encompass the whole wide world
Jesus has a great big heart
To love those who walk this earth.

Jesus has prepared a place
In the heavens above
A special room for each one of us
Given to us with His great love.

Jesus reaches down to earth
Like a beacon beaming in light
Saving us from the fiercest storm
Guiding us on the darkest night.

Jesus, Teacher, Counsellor, Friend
Came to save us from sin
And when He died it was not the end
But time for a new life to begin.

In my Father's house are many rooms, if it were not so, I would have told you. I am going there to prepare a place for you.
(John 14:2)

Jesus Gives Us

Jesus gives us His brightest light
To penetrate the darkest night
Guiding each one of us every day
Listening to our prayers when we pray.

Jesus gives us in abundance - gifts
To strengthen the Body and help us to live
With His peace as soft as clouds so white
He keeps us safe throughout day and night.

Jesus gives us 'Joy' with outstretched wings
The sweetest songs to celebrate and sing
His love warming us like the summer sun
As it beams down reaching everyone.

That at the name of Jesus every knee should bow. In every heaven and on earth and under the earth and tongue confess that Jesus Christ is Lord to the glory of God the Father.

(Philippians 2:10-11)

I BELIEVE THE greatest love of all is shown to us by God who gave His son, and Jesus who suffered so much for each one of us - such was His great sacrificial love. (Greater love has no-one than this, that he lay down his life for his friends - John 15:13).

Would any of us, however much we loved, be prepared to die in such humiliating circumstances! Jesus knew He would be betrayed by those close to Him, He knew He would suffer on the cross and yet Jesus said, "Father forgive them, for they do not know what they are doing" (Luke 23:34).

Would You Die

Would you die
For those you loved
Jesus died
For each one of us.

Would you die
To save a child's life
Jesus died
To bring us life.

Would you die
To save the world's sin
Jesus died
That we might live.

Would you die
To save another's loss
Jesus died
Upon a crude cross.

But he was pierced for our transgressions he was crushed for our iniquities. the punishment that brought us peace was upon him and by his wounds we are healed.

(Isaiah 53:5)

The Pathway to God

When sin met with love
Love's arms opened wide
And a Father's heart bled
As He was crucified.
So great was His love
That man's sins were forgiven
And a pathway to God
Was opened into heaven.

When love danced with Angels
In the heavens above
And Jesus had returned
To His own Father God
The pathway was laid
By hands made of love
For those who believed
In the purity of God
So that God's chosen children
Could be guided along
Following in the footsteps
Of Jesus, God's son.

Closing Chapter

WE ATTENDED BISHOP Titus's funeral on 27 February 2002 at Ruach Ministries Christian Centre, 122 Brixton Hill. There were so many radiant faces there, well over 700 people brought together by this one man, which was a tribute in itself. Many Bishops, clergy and members of his Churches along with friends, brothers, sisters and many who had flown in from Nigeria and America especially to take part in this final ceremony for this much-loved man. The finest tribute was the one written by Titus's wife, Aderonke. It touched many hearts and spoke so lovingly and truthfully of this amazing man.

A Tribute for Titus by his loving wife, Ronke

Olugbenga, the son of David was a man after God's own heart. As a lover of God, his desire was that all those who believed in Christ would love one another and be united as one even as the Father and Son are one.

He commended himself in every way in great endurance; in troubles, hardships, and distresses; in hard work, sleepless nights and hunger; in purity, understanding, patience and kindness; in the Holy Spirit and in sincere love; in truthful speech and in the power of God; through glory and dishonour; bad report and good report; genuine, yet regarded as an impostor; known, yet regarded as unknown; sorrowful, yet always rejoicing; poor yet making many rich; having nothing, and yet possessing everything, dead, and yet he lives on.

There were many other tributes given at the funeral and I made some notes on that day. Here is a summary of them.

"He was a gentle man of love and people loved him - truly a man of the people."

The gentleman who gave this tribute told the following story. They had been together for a gathering, and everyone had to sleep on the floor. Titus had been offered a bed which was more suited to his status as Bishop, but he replied, "Let me sleep on the floor with the people."

"He was a man of grace with great compassion. A man of unity, wanting to unite the whole world into one Body Of Christ. He built lasting relationships, and he was a leader who reached out in such a powerful way with his kind loving spirit."

"Titus was a soldier of the cross who had been snatched from us. He had broken barriers and removed boundaries, but his strong faith in God meant that he finished well. His body had been destroyed by someone, but they had not destroyed his spirit. We may grieve at the side of Titus's body that had been his home, but Titus the occupant was no longer there; he had gone to his heavenly home. His work has been completed in the eyes of God, but his work will still continue through those he leaves behind."

We were privileged to have known Titus and to be at his funeral on that special day. We were blessed and could feel the warmth of God's love and His presence with us at that sad time.

After the funeral service, Richard and I were shown to a KICC minibus that transported us, amongst others, to Camberwell New Cemetery, Brenchley gardens, SE23. It was a grey overcast day as we approached the cemetery. I remember thinking "Wouldn't it be wonderful if we were to see a rainbow in the sky," but then I thought, "that would be impossible because there is no sign of sunshine or rain."

The burial was touching, and we sang to the accompaniment of a single trumpet, "Abide With Me" and "Sleep On Beloved" and just as the last lines of the final hymn were being sung, I saw gentle raindrops fall onto my hymn sheet. As we finished singing the skies opened and brilliant sunshine reached down to us. Amazingly my prayers were answered as a colourful rain- bow shone in the sky just for a few minutes before it vanished as quickly as it came but instantly another appeared for a brief moment. I felt that God had shown His special sign to reveal that He was with us.

As we started to move away, I saw a pretty yellow freesia lying in the mud. It had been badly crushed and I bent down to pick it up for a souvenir of the day, and as I did so the main flower head dropped to the ground. I was left holding a very strong stem festooned with buds. I felt God speak to me and He said, "The beautiful flower has fallen, but the stem and buds are strong". I felt it was a message telling me that although Titus had gone, those coming behind were strong and would continue the work that he had started. I spoke to a member of Christ's Family Church explaining that I had this strong feeling that something good would grow out of this. He told me that others had also felt this very strongly,

Goodness would grow from this sadness.

Blossoms In The Mud

As I stood solemnly at the side of the grave
I saw a beautiful blossom lying in the mud
And as I picked up the yellow freesia that day
The flowerhead fell leaving the stem and buds.

God whispered to me - I heard His words
"Remember each blossom is here to play its
This flower has bloomed here on earth
And now it's time for the buds to start."

Jesus was once a beautiful blossom
And when He had played out His amazing role
He left behind the strong Spirit of love
To continue God's plan on earth for each soul.

RICHARD AND I settled into the minibus once again to the refrains of some wonderful uplifting Christian music that the driver had put on for us to listen to. As we drove through parts of London that I had never been to before, we enjoyed the colourful Spring flowering trees that shone out of the gardens and parks, as well as the beautiful daffodils and forsythia that lit up the day with colour.

We soon arrived at the reception, which was held at New Cross, London SE15, and many more tributes were read out in praise of Titus. Richard and I enjoyed meeting some old friends from Christ's Family Church and the Revd. Ayo Obayori who looked after us so well, making sure that someone was there to take us to Waterloo Station for our journey back to Berkshire. This very kind couple were so good to us. I do not even know their names to thank them on this page.

There were many others whose faces we knew and so many kindnesses were shown to us on that day. I thank everyone who was kind to us.

On the way home, Richard and I read again the words from the funeral "Order of Service" that had touched us and I felt it was appropriate to include in this chapter those beautiful words that were, I believe, favourite words of Titus.

I'm Free!

Don't grieve for me for I am free
I'm following the path God chose for me
I took His hand when I heard His call,
I turned my back and left it all

I could not stay another day
to laugh, to love, to work or play
Tasks left undone must stay that way
I found the place at the close of day
If my parting has left a void,
then fill it with remembered joy
A friendship shared, a laugh, a kiss
Oh yes these things I too will miss
Be not burdened with times of sorrow,
I wish you the sunshine of tomorrow
Perhaps my time seems all too brief;
Don't lengthen it now with undue grief
Lift up your heart and sing with me
God wanted me now, He set me free!
- ANON

WE REMINISCED ON the day as we remembered the beautiful rainbows.

I have set my rainbow in the clouds and it will be a sign of the covenant between me and the earth.
(Genesis 9:13)

Later I wrote this poem.

Remembering God's Rainbows

Rainbows kissed daffodils
Amidst gentle showers
Cherry trees blossomed
With the purest white flowers
So much sadness and love
On that February day
With prayers sent to God
So many words to say
God's beautiful rainbows
Brought heaven to earth
With glory and radiance
To colour our world.
Sweet loving memories
For us to take away
Remembering God's rainbows
On that special day.

THIS DAY HAD been very special to us, as it had been to others. It was a beautiful day filled with God's Spirit of peace and love. There was sadness, but also joy for Titus who had finished his life well. We knew he had gone home to be with his Father in heaven.

I dedicate this poem to the memory of Bishop Titus Olugbenga David.

Breathe softly sweet child

Breath from fragrant clouds
Filled with the sweetness of God
As His gentle wings of love
Reach down to your soft cheeks
And harmony reigns with peace
God's gentleness is like gossamer
And the soft petals of fresh flowers.

Breathe sweetly 'chosen child'
As rainbows of the purest light
Free you from earthly world
Into the strong arms of God
Gentle raindrops like melodies play
As soft sleep comes to end the day
Lost in God's comforting caress
Silent sleep as Angels bless.

For I am convinced that neither death nor life, neither angels nor demons, neither the present nor the future, nor any powers, neither height nor depth, nor anything else in all creation, will be able to separate us from the love of God, that is in Christ Jesus our Lord.

(Romans 8:38-39)

The Lord bless you and keep you. The Lord make His face shine upon you and be gracious to you. The Lord turn His face towards you and give you peace.

(Numbers 6:24-26)

About The author

YVONNE WAS BORN in Staines Middlesex and spent her early years growing up in London, where she received a restricted education due to wartime bombing, shortages and lack of facilities.

She moved with her parents to Surrey in 1956 where she was able to enjoy the freedom of the countryside, especially riding her horse and driving her pony and trap.

Yvonne met her husband Richard in 1959 and they were married in 1964 choosing to continue living in Surrey until they moved into Berkshire in 1982 where they still live.

Yvonne achieved her lifetime ambition to teach in 1970 and received the gift of creative writing and poetry soon after she was born again.

Printed in Great Britain
by Amazon

47130429R00076